Maria Dek

A Walk in the Forest

PRINCETON ARCHITECTURAL PRESS · NEW YORK

In the forest, wonders await...

...as countless as the trees.

It's the best playground ever.

Run wild in the jungle!

In the forest,
you can shout as loud as you want.

Follow footprints.

See where they lead you.

Look!

Find treasure.

Flowers and feathers, pinecones and stones, a lizard's tail.

All is small in the forest.

All is big.

And deep.

Wade in.

The birds have secrets. So do the trees. Listen!

You might meet a fox. Just be patient.

The forest is full of burrows, hollows, and nests.
Every animal has its own hiding place.

Build a shelter. Play hide and seek.

When night falls in the forest, it is magical.

And maybe a little scary, too.

You'll go there tomorrow, when you're older.

Published by
Princeton Architectural Press
A McEvoy Group company
202 Warren Street
Hudson, New York 12534

Visit our website at www.papress.com

First published in France under the title
En forêt by Marcel & Joachim.
Marcel & Joachim © 2015

English edition © 2017 Princeton Architectural Press
All rights reserved
Printed and bound in China
20 19 18 17   5 4 3 2

ISBN 978-1-61689-569-3

This book was hand illustrated by the author with
watercolor applied with a brush.

Design: Clément Chassagnard

For Princeton Architectural Press:
Editor: Nicola Brower

Special thanks to: Janet Behning, Abby Bussel,
Erin Cain, Tom Cho, Barbara Darko, Benjamin English,
Jenny Florence, Jan Cigliano Hartman, Lia Hunt,
Mia Johnson, Valerie Kamen, Simone Kaplan-Senchak,
Stephanie Leke, Diane Levinson, Jennifer Lippert, Kristy Maier,
Sara McKay, Jaime Nelson Noven, Rob Shaeffer,
Sara Stemen, Paul Wagner, Joseph Weston, and
Janet Wong of Princeton Architectural Press
—Kevin C. Lippert, publisher

Library of Congress Cataloging-in-Publication Data
available upon request.